Dominik

Olivia

Olivia

Pascal

Siria

Silvan

Karin

Lea

Luca

Troy

Wishes by Adrian, Ambra, Claudio, Daniel, Daniela, Denise, Dominik, Fiona,
Gian, Jonas, Lea, Luca, Nico, Olivia, Olivia, Pascal, Siria, Silvan, Troy
Wishes selected by Päivi Stalder

First published in the United States, Great Britain, Canada, Australia, and
New Zealand in 2010 by North-South Books Inc., an imprint of NordSüd Verlag AG,
CH-8005 Zürich, Switzerland.
Distributed in the United States by North-South Books Inc., New York 10001.

Library of Congress Cataloging-in-Publication Data is available.
Printed in Belgium by Proost N.V., B 2300 Turnhout, April 2010.
ISBN: 978-0-7358-2331-0 (trade edition)
1 3 5 7 9 • 10 8 6 4 2

www.northsouth.com

FSC
Mixed Sources
Product group from well-managed
forests and other controlled sources
Cert no. BV-COC-070303
www.fsc.org
© 1996 Forest Stewardship Council

My Wish Tonight

★WHAT CHILDREN WISH

ILLUSTRATED BY
Iris Wolfermann

NorthSouth
New York / London

I wish tonight that everyone has a job they like.

I wish that my guinea pigs will live forever.

I wish that I'll get a baby tiger—a **real** one.

I wish that my dad will play soccer with me every day,
even when I'm all grown up.

I wish that my sister won't
argue with me anymore.

I wish that everything
was made of chocolate.

I wish that everybody in the world
has a home.

I wish that people would take more care of the environment.

I wish I could have a tractor and a trailer and a cow.

And a chain so the cow won't fall out.

I wish that during the night nobody has an accident.

I wish that my brother isn't allergic to cats anymore.

I wish that I could fly to Mars
and look for alien bones.

I wish my turtle that the fox took
would come back.

I wish that I could sit on a cloud
and look at the stars.

I wish I could go faster than the speed of sound.

Then I'd get to school in less than a minute.

I wish that angels will protect me in the dark.

I wish that my granny can *see* again.

I wish that the moon doesn't lose me when I sleep.

I wish that I could ride to school on a horse.

I wish that all the children in the world
sleep well.

Wishes by:

Fiona

Adrian

Ambra

Claudio

Gian

Daniel

Jonas

Denise

Daniela